VICTORY OVER FORGIVENESS

VICTORY OVER FORGIVENESS

HELEN E. CUMBO

authorHOUSE®

AuthorHouse™
1663 Liberty Drive
Bloomington, IN 47403
www.authorhouse.com
Phone: 1-800-839-8640

Published by AuthorHouse   03/01/2013

ISBN: 978-1-4817-1897-4 (sc)
ISBN: 978-1-4817-1898-1 (e)

Dedication

This book is dedicated to my inspiring and encouraging friend, Marvin, who told me not to give up completing my book. To my wonderful, patient neighbor, Jan Thomas, who typed my manuscript for publication. With God's strength He has made all this possible.

FIRST LET ME tell you of my childhood. It was a world of fantasy and a world of loneliness. I lived in the country with my grandmother, my mother's mother. Grandma as I called her was a medium height, round, light skinned teacher and principal. I loved to hear the stories of how she and grandfather traveled by wagon to school. She taught three grades in one, big, cold room. The joy she had in teaching and helping boys and girls, instilled in me the desire to teach. Her mother was a white lady with blond Shirley Temple curls whose picture hung on the wall in a large picture frame.

She told me the story of how this ten room house was added on room by room by my grandfather and her. It stood on over 45 acres of land.

My grandfather's huge picture hung on the wall also by my grandma's bed. It looked so huge to me as a child. It was 20 by 30 inches high.

I was told that I was a very bad child who had fits of anger and who fought for her rights. I had no one to protect me.

The house in which I grew up had lots of rooms with high ceilings and a long rolling staircase. I love to climb the stairs and slide down the banisters. This was fun for me for I had very few amusements. What I enjoyed most in the evenings or snowy weather, was to listen to Grandma read from books about the flood destroying the world and looking at those horrible pictures of women, children, and men with mouth opened, fighting for their lives in the huge waves of water. She said, "The next time the world would be destroyed by fire". I then could see in my mind people screaming in the blazes of fire.

I would then be a part of those scenes, my grandmother and I fighting to keep our heads above the rushing waters. I would want to find out more about it, yet I was deeply afraid inside. She would then talk to me about drinking alcohol. The pictures in the book had men before drinking and after drinking looking like beasts from consuming a great deal of alcohol. My grandmother had a library of many exciting books and I enjoyed living those lives of different characters she read to me.

My grandmother was the backbone of the community. She knew what happened back then for she was a part of the history making. She was involved with the girl scouts which came to our yard many evenings to hear stories my grandma told. I grew up in a community with my grandma in a big ten room house, just two of us, which she said she and her husband built. The community was called Wadsworth and our church was named after the great writer and poet, Henry Wadsworth Longfellow. During those early years there were about 60 or 70 members all black and they are linked through Madison Lindsay, who founded the church in 1870. I grew up with a picture of the couple hanging on the wall in my Grandma Libby's living room. She gave the picture to the Wadsworth Congregation Church which hangs in the church today.

I will never forget the time that I had to get up in front of the congregation and recite one of Longfellow's poems, Paul Revere's ride, whose opening line, "Listen my children and you shall hear". I grew up in a world of history and excitement especially when my Grandma Libby told me many things that happened back then and I regret I can't remember them all. She also told of the one room schoolhouse where she taught school to the children and my Grandfather Wayne was a distinguished principal of the county. The school was not far from the church and it was torn down in the late 1930s which my grandmother tried to stop. My grandmother put electricity in the old church and was a faithful member in the community until her death. Now the Wadsworth congregation church has recently been designated as a historic property by the county commissioners.

Winters in the country with strongly and snowy weather kept plenty of air penetrating through the cracks which kept the house cold. It was very hard on grandma and me. Early in the mornings I would pull out wood from a blanket of snow and cut most of it with an ax. I would have the bedroom warm by the time grandma awoke. I could not understand why my uncle, grandma's son, who lived nearby didn't come down to check on us to see if we were all right. Even his children didn't come down to give me a hand or to help to draw water from the well. I loved to cook on top of the stove in the bedroom and make hoe cake. It was made of shortening, flour, and milk and cooked slowly on each side until it rose. It was my favorite in the mornings with butter and syrup on our plates. Later after cleaning dishes and making the bed grandma and I shared, I would listen to the radio. I had a great imagination when my favorite story of the Phantom Knows came on. It sounded so real and I could see everything I heard on the radio in my mind. All through the years as a child my mind had matured for most of my life was spent in imagining things and important things I wanted to do when I became older.

There were beautiful days in this big 10 room house, many places to hide and explore and make believe. I enjoyed trying on my mother's silver shoes and especially a red, beautiful sequined dress. There were beautiful experiences while playing up stairs alone and making believe.

As time passes, I learned I was three years old when my mother passed. She had grandma promise that she would keep me and not my father.

My grandma was very protective of me with my father. When my father came from the big city of Charleston to see me and other relatives once in a while, grandma would not let me go off with him. So I never met my Cousins whom were descendants of Cherokee Indians.

My grandmother introduced me to the magazine Wee Wisdom when I was very young. It arrived every month with all types of activities for young children to do. It taught you about God and His wonders, poems, and exciting stories. I loved this magazine as a child and I'm sure I almost saved every issue. In my classroom when teaching the months of the year, I cut the covers from my old Wee Wisdom magazines and printed the months in large letters under each picture. Looking at them above the chalkboard gave me a lot of happy memories back when I was a child.

Grandma also loved these affirmations and also because they were Charles Fillmore's favorites.

The joy of the Lord is your strength.
God in me is infinite wisdom. He shows me what to do.
In all thy way acknowledge Him, and He will direct thy path.
I can do all things through Christ which strengthens me.
All things work together for good.
In quietness and in confidence shall be your strength.
Faith is the strength of the soul inside and lost is the man without it.
The greatest teaching ever given is:
"Christ in you, the hope of glory" (Col. 1:27)
"God is my help in every need" is a passage I would say to
myself when I needed strength to carry out a project, or any other
stressful activity.

I experienced great amusement and satisfaction as I played out in the big park in front of our house. The roots which grew out of the ground served as my kitchen, bedroom, and living room. I had a little green and white tin stove and I would make believe I was making a pie and would pull down the oven door and slide it inside. Those were wonderful, peaceful times I experienced as I played and dreamed alone.

Going to school on the big orange bus was fun and excitement for me. Being in the lower grades meant we sat in the center of the bus and the larger kids on each side of us. Pretty soon, I was afraid and didn't want to ride the bus. The big kids, including my third cousin Myrtle would snatch my hat off and throw it to each other.

Myrtle was very fair skinned with dark brown hair. Myrtle lived with her family right across the way from grandma's house. Her grandmother, Maggie and three brothers grew up with her and protected her. I had no one and I had to learn quick how to protect myself. I had been pushed, picked on, called names, etc. when I was younger by Myrtle and her brothers, and now I decided it's time to put a stop to it.

One day in the park in front of my grandma's house, Myrtle said, "I dare you to cross over this line, blackie". So she drew a line on the ground. I stepped over the line, grabbed her by her hair and drug her out of the park kicking and screaming, calling for her grandmother. Her grandmother came running with a broom after me, telling me to "turn her a loose, you devil". Well, that ended that for I didn't have to prove myself to her again.

Myrtle and I became very close in our teenage years. We would walk over two or three miles to catch the bus to the city. We never had to catch a bus back home for we always had someone to drive us back.

I would always feel sorry for Myrtle when her mother would put her down and making little hurtful remarks like" why don't you dress like Lucinda. Look how nice her dress looks". This continued on into Myrtle's adult life, when she married. Myrtle's husband and child were too dark for her mother and were never accepted.

I often wondered if God had given Myrtle's mother all dark children rather than light, what would she have done?

I would find great comfort in a beautiful bed that grandma said my mother had bought for me as a little child. The only bed I had ever slept in. I suppose you could call it a youth bed to grow with a child. Many years later during my childhood I found myself cuddle up wishing that my mother was here with me to comfort me or just to feel her arms around me. Losing a mother at a very early stage of one's life can manifest many emotional problems.

Growing up in the country with grandma was exciting and experimental. I was in charge of the whole ten room house and I enjoyed cooking, cleaning, washing, and taking care of grandma.

There was a lot of work to be done on the house because it had been standing for over 100 years. I got up on the stove to reach the high ceilings when I painted. The iceman came sometimes and sometimes he didn't. I dreamed of the luxury of a refrigerator and when I got a job in the city at Marie's grille, the first thing on my list was to buy a white refrigerator. It was the first frig to be in our community.

My early childhood and being alone at school, I didn't have any self-esteem. My grandma provided for me the best as she could and didn't receive any money from my dad for support. I went to school with shoes sewn by Grandma to hold the soles together and wore my mother's green and red swim suits as undershirts after she cut the shorts off. Yes I was picked on and made fun of but still I tried to show everyone that it didn't hurt me as I became older.

Instead of staying in the background, I ventured out and became very popular at school. I participated in skits on stage and even wore my mother's beautiful red sequin gown as I portrayed Lena Horn and sang "Stormy Weather."

As years went by I became very interested in drama. The play, "Pink and Patches", was a big hit and we were invited to other high schools to perform. We went to my cousin's high school and make a big hit with the students. The play seemed to portray my life, having no material things. I did receive hand-me-downs from my city cousins which I truly appreciated. The main remark in the play was, "Hit don't make no real difference". The students repeated this slang to the teachers. The teachers would answer by saying, "if you don't have the assignment, hit will make a difference." That year I received a medal for best actress in drama.

I was involved in 4-H Club helping grandma can fruit and vegetables to carry to the fair. I will never forget the time my little calf was presented by me at age 13. The girls were to stay in a building on a farm and boys in the barn with the calves and cows. Seeing how the boys picked at my little calf, I decided to sleep next to her so she would be safe. Each boy was to walk around a circle leading their animal and so did I. My grandma Libby was so proud of me when I received a prize and a letter from North Carolina Mutual Life Insurance Company and an article in the newspaper. I felt so proud and happy. I did receive blue ribbons from 4-H Club for canning fruits and having the cleanest house in the community.

I was the first Negro girl in the county to participate in an affair like this which was September 21, 1945. The following is a letter I received from Mr. C.C. Spalding, president of Mutual Life Insurance Company.

This is the way grandma spoke of sex. When I became a woman I didn't know what was wrong with me. One boy put his hand on my shoulder and I slapped him. He was very angry and asked why. I told him my grandma said, "Don't let boys put their hands on you." On the night Perry would come calling, I was so frightened that I begged Grandma to answer the door.

As the years rolled by I grew more attractive with long, thick, black hair. The boys liked me and wanted to have a date with me. The girls would be angry with me when my hair moved as I turned my head. I was very careful to hold my neck so my hair wouldn't fly around. I wanted to be friends with the other girls.

I rode with my Uncle Tom to town which was an exciting experience. On many occasions I carried vegetables, corn, and collard greens to sell at the local markets and bunches of daffodils grouped in twelve and wrapped with a tie. I would save the vegetable money to buy a 10¢ loaf of bread for grandma and me and my favorite sweet was a honey bun 5¢ each. I loved going to town see my aunt M, Olivia, Richard, Patrick, and Janice.

When I grew a few years older, I heard from my first Cousins who lived not far away, discussing a movie they had seen the night before. I didn't quite understand what a movie was. Oh how I ached to go with them to such a place but was never asked. Years passed and one day I told my uncle my desire to see a movie. He drove me to town to my city cousin's house and told me that I would have time to go to a movie and the time he would return to pick me up.

This was an exciting day for me. Olivia and Monica who were my older cousins took me to a place called Palace Theaters. In all of this huge screen I saw men riding on horses and a big, long thing which was a train that was coming through the screen towards me. I jumped up and screamed, "Take me out; I don't want that thing to run over me." Olivia put her hands over my mouth and said "Shut up, they will put us out." I continued to yell, "Let me out, Uncle Tom is waiting for me. I hear him blowing his car horn." They became so angry with me that we all left the theater. The experience I longed to see turned out to be a horrible nightmare.

Later in school I became a fighter. I had no one to protect or look out for me, not even my Cousins whom I protected from fights. As I sat in class, sometimes I would dream of New York City, acting on a big stage.

I went to visit my dad at 11 or 12 years old with my two Cousins. We wore big tags around our necks with names and address printed on them. Yes, I was very afraid to venture out.

My stepmother was exactly like the mean one in storybooks, only worse. She disliked me from the beginning in the way she treated me and I was afraid to eat or drink at her house. My dad would say, "It's all right for you to eat because I cooked it." My visit to the big city was not a happy time. I never understood why my stepmother hated me so much. I had nothing to do with my dad having two wives before her.

I had eczema on my hands as a young child and my stepmother's son and daughter had it in the creases of their arms, behind their knees, and on their hands also. One morning when she saw me putting ointment on my hands she said, "What's that on your hands, you must have a bad disease?" I walked up to her as she backed away, I said, "I'll beat the hell out of you if you ever accuse me of that." She continued to back off from me and my dad had a smile on his face. I never heard that remark again on future trips to the city.

A few days after my cousin, Olivia's marriage she and her husband were to leave for the city. Knowing this, my grandmother arranged for me to go with them and therefore I would not be on the train alone. It was a long trip but I looked out of the window and slept a lot.

We finally arrived at an aunt of my cousin's husband. It was my first time to eat oyster stew and I found myself liking it very much. We stayed overnight with the in-laws and left for the city the next day.

I did get to visit my cousin Olivia since we weren't too far away from each other as I visited my dad. Her husband was originally from the island, a tall, good looking guy. He was a great photographer and took my picture while in the city and later when my children were infants (he took pictures of them in their diapers).

My cousin was excited about her marriage and told me of the excitement she experienced when he took her to Jamaica. She said, "she was like a queen." Everyone waited on her in every way and even wanted to bathe her. She said that's when she drew the line.

Time passed along while visiting with my cousin and her new husband. I thought he was a very nice person until he grabbed me one day. I fought to be let loose and he said, "You know I have a lot to lose if you tell Olivia." I promised that I would not tell if he promised not to bother me again. I kindly stayed away when he was in town and visited my cousin when I knew she was alone.

I do remember sitting in her kitchen window three or four stories high up, being introduced to Pall Mall cigarettes at age 16. I became so dizzy and sick that I could have fallen out of the window. That was my first addiction to smoking.

Many years went by and Olivia and husband bought a beautiful home. They had many friends and partied mostly every weekend in their basement. They never had children after Olivia found out she had a medical problem and could not bring a child to term. They were very distraught and sad knowing this.

Down the line, the marriage began to fall apart with infidelities, affairs, etc. so they were divorced. Olivia bought his half of the property and she stayed in the house until she met her second husband. His wife died and he was left with two children. He had a good administrative job in the next town.

When I met him, his sisters, brother and other members of his family, seemed to have a very strong family tie. I felt she had gotten a very nice person.

When my husband and I bought a home in the same state, I found myself calling my cousin Olivia and she never called. Her husband told me one day that he ask her "Why don't you call Lucinda?" She would always say "I will when I have time." Her weekend would always be very busy with her so called friends. She would prepare food and drinks for her downstairs parties which would last until the wee hours in the morning. This was a weekend tradition. The friends were always there to party but when there were crisis, they were not always there.

I remember when I called and asked the two of them if I could come over because I just had to get away from home and talk to someone. They were very kind and offered me a place to stay upstairs.

While Olivia was at work, I decided I would go to the store and get something nice for dinner and have it all ready when she arrived at home from work. Well, she didn't seem too pleased. I thought that working all day and traveling home by train and bus would give her opportunity to rest.

I would stay in my room and go to sleep with giggles, loud voices, and music. I was not in the same mood as her guests to party.

One day after cleaning the house, I went upstairs to take a nap since no one was home from work. I was awakened by Olivia's husband lying on my back. I awoke, pushed him off and stood up. I told him how disappointed I was in him and how highly I felt about him. I said, "All of you guys are alike."

Yes, you guessed it-it was time for me to leave and so I did. I never said a word about the incident until many years later, when I confided in Margie and Aunt Libby and they died never telling a soul.

With blessing and joy I think back to the days past and very happy with my decision to dissolve the relationship with my first husband the cab driver.

While on the college campus, I met this tall, good looking, and light skinned guy. He drove a cab and lived with his blind, alcoholic mother. I guess I fell in love with him because we were very compatible and I loved being with him. He didn't allow me to have alcoholic drinks and he hated drinking. His mother, an alcoholic, tried to keep it hidden from him, but deep down: I believed he knew about it. When I would go over to his house unannounced, there would be her male friends in the living room drinking with her. Naturally, he met and knew a lot of people being a cab driver especially women in our city and later I found out that I had competition with another girl whose name was the same as mine. He had been dating her before I met him, so I continued to see him. He had my Grandmother fascinated and fooled with him. He would go to the country to see her and bring her gifts and she would fix him dinner. She liked him a lot. I felt so dirty and felt that I had betrayed my Grandmother since she raised me to be a good girl. I talked this over with my friend and he said we could go out of state and get married but we must keep our marriage a secret.

One night at my Aunt's house where I lived off campus, I told my first cousin that I wasn't going to school tomorrow because we were getting married. I told her not to tell anyone because it was a secret.

We did go and we were married in a lady's house who he knew in South Carolina. I was so nervous that I had my period. The lady told me to drink some vinegar and that would stop it.

We finally told Grandma of our marriage and on weekends we could freely visit her in the country. This man was very controlling and didn't want me around certain people and mainly wanted control over my life.

I remember we would go out of town to see a big band and to dance and when we arrived; he would say you can go into the dance. I'll stay in the car. I didn't want him disappointed by not seeing his famous musicians, so I volunteered to sit in the car. I sat hours and hours into the early morning until it was over. Not once did he come out to check on me; to see if I was safe or okay. I made up my mind that I must get out of this mess for good.

He had me so mixed up that I withdrew from college and went to New York and got a job at Dewars on 34th as a hostess. Leaving my grandma and going to New York to work, to clear my mind, and save money to go back to college was very exhilarating. I loved the excitement, the tall buildings, and the new experiences of city life. This city life made a deep impression on me compared to the dull life I had experienced all my life. It was wonderful having indoor plumbing and running water. My aunt with whom I lived gave me no restrictions on what I should or shouldn't do. In other words, she had confidence of what Grandma had instilled in me, so she trusted me.

My next plan after getting settled in this big, exciting city was to save my money for college. My stepmother knew of a modeling job downtown New York. She volunteered to take me. When the guy became very interested in signing me up she said, "We'll think about it" and we left. She explained that she didn't like the surroundings and he may try to molest me. I never tried that again because it made me very nervous just thinking what might have taken place.

My Aunt Beulah read in the papers one morning about the hiring at a huge restaurant on 34th Street called Dewars. She was familiar with the area and the clientele. I was interviewed and got the job. I was to stand by the entrance and welcome patrons in and seat them. The other girls were busing tables, etc. One wanted to know how I was able to get the job. She said, "Maybe it's your looks and long hair." I did make it pretty well with Zoie who was an attractive, olive skinned girl who was employed there. I liked her very much and we got along very well together.

After working at Dewars for months, the manager approached Zoie and I for weekend jobs which paid very good. Naturally, we took it. We served food in beautiful homes and stacked up what was left and it was picked up. We enjoyed working but it took away our weekends but we didn't mind.

Zoie invited me to her apartment which was small and not very attractive. Before I left to go back to Brooklyn, she would tell me that she had cramps and when her man came home he would rub her stomach to make the pain go away. I never met any of her male friends.

I enjoyed my job which made me leave early in the morning when the sun was just coming up. I rode the subway but my aunt gave me a pair of scissors to keep in my purse for protection. Nothing ever took place during my employment in New York.

On many occasions I noticed this policeman in the restaurant every morning trying to make eye contact with me. I thought nothing of it until he approached me. He said, "You haven't been working here too long because this is my beat." I told him when I started and left it at that. The conversations continued later and one day he wanted to know my name and where I lived. He said just be careful when riding the subways.

Weeks went by and he didn't come in. I figured they had changed his work location. Finally, he came back and found me. He had a package all wrapped up and said, "I have something for you." I said, "What is it?" He told me to open it after work. I couldn't wait to see what was inside and when I did, I found the most fantastic outfit I had ever seen. I will never forget it as long as I live for I can visualize it today. My wardrobe was very limited for my aunt would let me wear some of her outfits now and then. The skirt was flair of red and black design, the blouse was black with a huge flower made of the skirt material (red and black). What was so strange was the fact it fit me perfectly. The gifts continued to come but he never got out of line with me. My aunt talked to me and said be careful.

On one evening as I was leaving the restaurant, he came up to me and said, "I'll ride with you until you get home." He was Caucasian, tall, good looking, older than I, probably seven to ten years older. As I'm riding home I'm wondering what will my family say. When we arrived in front of the brownstone, I didn't ask him in but I did thank him for bringing me home.

I met other young people and finally, I met Bill. He was a friend of my aunt's and we had a couple of dates. He was very nice and took me to nice places to eat in New York. While walking down the street we would pass jewelry stores and the like. He stopped in front of this jewelry and said, "Pick out what you like." I did, and I still have the ring today. It looks as good as it did when I was eighteen years old. On another occasion, he bought me a necklace. He was a very nice person but I didn't love him, I only liked him as a friend. Before I broke up with him, I never knew if he was a woman or a man because he treated me with respect.

Soon I met a guy called T. He was exciting and we both enjoyed each other. He knew the ropes of city life and what he had he thought he owned. He was so controlling of me and I didn't care for that because I didn't belong to anyone at that time.

He became so hung up with me that when I told him I was returning home he said, "No! You are not leaving." That evening he came to my aunt's house with a gun and that's when my aunt got into the picture. She had a very serious talk with T and finally made him understand.

After returning back home from New York many years later, my aunt wrote me that diabetes had taken one of Bill's legs and he wasn't doing well. I felt for him because he was such a kind and generous person.

Enrolling back in college and getting settled back into completing my education, I met Vavilier while out in a club with my cousin. He knew my cousin and asked him to introduce us. They were in high school together.

I will never forget when my grandma met Vavilier for the first time. She looked straight into his eyes and said, "You are a very sneaky person!" I was so embarrassed, yet I didn't know at that time she was so right. Coming home for the holidays from college, I would cook my favorite dish, chicken and dumplings, and when he would leave for the long ride to the city, I would stand at the window crying and feeling so alone. I never had a father figure in my life and I wanted this feeling to be filled by having him. He would tell me how he was working two jobs to get me this blue diamond and I would get it when he came for Valentine's Day. Our relationship went on for some time and he made many trips back and forth from New York.

We were married my junior year in college and my oldest child was born in March of the next year before my graduation. I attended college up to the last day before I gave birth to a beautiful baby. She was baptized on the college campus and the college organist and wife were her God-parents. I only took leave for two weeks and returned back to college for final exams and my graduation. That was a very happy day for me and a very joyous grandma, for I was the fourth generation to finish from this college, which was a woman's college when I attended. When Grandpa, Grandma, aunts, and mother attended this school, it was a co-ed school. I had my first teaching position with eleven other teachers in a brand new school. I loved it there and when my daughter was school age, she attended school with me.

Some years later, my first husband, the cab driver, would send me messages that he wanted to see me. I had no interest or desire to start a relationship with him. Maybe he also knew what other knew of my husband's infidelity at his school with the dietitian. Maybe this would teach Vavilier a lesson so I let it be known that the cab driver could call me at a certain time knowing that Vavilier would be home also. When he called, Vavilier listened on the extension phone and told him he had better not call here again with foul language and leave his wife alone.

This was after Vavilier heard my ex telling me how sorry he was that our marriage didn't work out and how he regretted the way he treated me for he really did love me and still does. He begged me to meet him so we could talk. I realized the affair was over so I left it at that—finished.

When my family was invited to attend my aunt and uncle's 50th wedding anniversary party I couldn't wait to return home for the big occasion. I would also get to see my daughter who at that time was in college.

People from out of town and everywhere would be there. Even the pastor and wife from the local church were invited.

It was a beautiful affair and Aunt M's oldest son officiated and opened the affair with a very nice speech about his parents.

We had plenty of delicious food, drink, and music. Everyone including myself let their hair down by having two or three cocktails. After the affair, we had breakfast at Aunt B's son's home. Most of us left the reception and didn't make it to the hotel and went right over in our outfits.

When I married my second husband, my dad and stepmother came to my home from the city. My dad told me that he would pay for my wedding cake. He didn't publicly say, "Lucinda this is money for your cake." He was watched so closely by his wife that he held my hand and the $20 bill was slipped in my hand. I am sorry that my dad wasn't man enough to say openly, "This is for your cake," however, he walked on eggshells around her.

On Dad's dying bed, he held my hand very tightly in his and said, "Lucinda, I know I didn't do right by you." I said, "That's in the past and over with."

When my husband's job required us to move, I found myself becoming anxious which was imminent within the family circle. As one would imagine it would involve adjustment, physical work, decisions, and added pressure. James 4:7 says that surrender empower the believer and forces the devil to flee. Once I submitted my mind and heart to what I had experienced and still experiencing, I was refreshed with God's peace that surround me. (Philippians 4:7)

Recruiters came to town just at a time, which would give us employment. In an unexpectedly short while everything was accomplished smoothly and easily without undue problems. We rented a very lovely furnished rock house with plenty of room and a huge fireplace in the living room.

Trust the spirit within us to give us the right ideas to strengthen ourselves and to heal us from limiting relationships. We can trust the spirit to bring us new peacefulness to our bodies and give us guidance in making big or little decisions.

I enjoyed my teaching position very much and I was concerned about the conditions of my pupils. By the time they became adjusted to school and began to learn, they would have to leave school and head for a new location. The parents were migrant workers and the children were in and out of many schools. It hurt me so much to see their little eyes shine and the living conditions when I made home visits and saw the dirt floor and one bedroom homes. My heart bled for them.

The experience was exciting and rewarding and I enjoyed my teaching very much. I became very friendly with the principal's daughter and visited her often and helped her out when she was ill. She had a prize relic car which you had to shift gears, which I had forgotten. She needed items from the grocer and I had no other transportation to get there. It was a miracle but I did continue to try and I was able to return back to her home.

I flew to Ft. Meyers to pack up my personal items and get furniture, which I was told I could have. The new king size bedroom suit, colonial kitchen set, and other items he wanted. I took the refinished bed of my grandma from my early childhood, the first bedroom suit and couch we got after marriage. I packed the boxes and sealed them with tape. The next day I went by to finish the loose ends and got furniture lined up to be moved. My boxes had been reopened and resealed.

My son-in-law had set up my move with a furniture friend who owed him a favor who drove out of state to pick up new furniture so he traveled empty.

My things arrived safely and I had a handy man, Andy, to come by to help the driver unload the furniture. I loved the house here with two acres of land and no snakes to worry about. We sold the house we had together and the monies were divided between my husband and me.

He called the guys who maintained his boat to help him move. When he arrived in Tennessee his furniture wasn't packed, it was tossed into the truck. His bike wheels were twisted sideways; his boxes opened all over the place and found his favorite black leather jacket which I gave him missing. He said it probably happened when they sent him out to get them beer. They really took him for a ride, especially when they charged him such high prices when working on the boat.

Things didn't go well in Tennessee and it became so bad that I had to put a lock on my bedroom door. My phone would be answered by him when I wasn't in. He would ask, "Who is this?" when my cousin, Johnny, would ask for me. He didn't catch Johnny's voice and told him not to call any damn more. Johnny later called me and said, "I thought you kept your door locked." I said, "I do." "Well he answered your phone." He had gotten in some way and rambled through all my personals.

He went ahead with his social life, buying Christmas gifts for his friends. I had had enough from him and I didn't want to be bothered so I asked him to leave.

One day when I was shopping in a market, I noticed this very attractive person looking and smiling at me. Something said here is your chance. He came up to me and introduced himself. I told him my first name. He wanted to know where I lived and my phone number. He called that same evening.

This was in the early 90's and since he was a professor at the local university, seemed very caring. I said why not. My little dog, Peanut, was very protective of me. He would always be between the two of us. He growled when my friend moved towards me. He was the perfect chaperone.

As time progressed and he came almost every day and brought lunch, also beer on his lunch time, I felt he was getting too close. We began to talk about ourselves and I asked, "Are you married?" He answered honestly, "Yes, but we aren't together." That just didn't go well with me. Although I had experienced that, been there, done that. It would be payback time so why should I be concerned. We would have dinner away from the city because of his students and this became exciting to me. He treated me very well and wanted me to go on trips occasionally to New York. I declined because my mind went back to a movie I had seen of two people, one married and the other a girlfriend and the plane went down. I just couldn't do it.

This affair went on until my cousin found out about him and told me to stay away from him. When he was in the army the Indian guys didn't want us to look at their women, let alone go out with them.

He became too progressive and I told him that this must end. He continued to call morning and evening and I said, "No." He knew where my cousin lived but not the address. He rode around until he saw my car. He rang the doorbell and I let him in. He met my cousin and her husband and also another cousin who happened to be there. I told him that I had met a loving and caring person who wasn't married and we didn't have to hide out. I also told him to go to his wife and straighten things out, just don't call me anymore. If you come around my home again there could be trouble. It was a lovely, quiet neighborhood and I didn't want any trouble. Even now, after all the years, I continually get calls from him.

Yes, the house was sold by "owner" and I had no trouble selling it. My cousins came over and helped take drapes down, checked the attic, and helped with packing. I bought my ex out and he left for Georgia. He wanted another chance to start over with me and spoke to the truck driver. His things were all packed on the truck and ready to go when the truck driver said, "I'll take everything off at no charge if you let him stay." I said, "Emphatically no! Keep his things on your truck." There was no turning back for I had waited over thirty some years to have some peace. It was finalized at last.

I heard later that he had met a woman from mail order from the Islands and was getting married. She was anxious to get to the USA and they soon relocated in the states, sometime later. My daughter told me that she was just a few years older than she.

My daughter called me to let me know that her father got on a plane and on his way to see me. She asked me to do her a favor by looking into assisted living arrangements and nursing homes he could go in to. I went to four or five living facilities and got prices, etc. to send to my daughter. Before we could make arrangements, they sent him to a facility about 45 miles away. He went with only the clothing on his back. I received another call from my daughter, "Mom", she says, "I hate to put you through this but will you go to the nursing home and pick up Daddy's belongings?" I did so because I felt sorry for him. I stopped by the next day to pick up his three suitcases, two or three bags with suits and winter clothes and all were packed with clean and soiled clothes all together and it took days to get the odor out of my car.

While at the nursing home he called me collect almost every day. He wanted me to come and bring our dog, Pee Nut. I did the following Sunday. When we arrived, he was on the back porch just staring out into space and he had lost a lot of weight and was wearing taped up eye glasses. He said the lady hit him and broke his glasses after he called her a name. He also stopped eating because he thought they put something in his food.

He needed medical treatment badly, so I got him an appointment and drove back to pick him up and drove to the doctor's office. We had a difficult time getting him out of the car and into a wheelchair. When his doctor saw him, he could not believe his eyes. The nurse said, "I'll help your father." "She's not my damned daughter, she's my wife" my ex-husband said.

Dr. Snow said that you should be awarded thinking about his health after he went to the Islands to get a wife and treated you the way he did. I told him that something went wrong for him to pack up and bring everything from the island. He wanted his TV but couldn't bring it on the plane. When he made the change in Korea, he became belligerent and they put him in jail overnight and next morning put him on a plane for the states. I don't see how he made it, walking on crutches with an open ankle wound.

Around another month, the children came home to help pack him up to go back to the Island. We drove down to the nursing home to pack up his belongings and then we finally got everything in the trunk and back seat. It was rather crowded but we made it. When we arrived back in town, I took everyone out to eat which he seemed to enjoy.

My daughter had hinted about him staying at my house but I declined. I made reservations at the motel where my daughter spent the night with him. The children took my car to pick up items for packing his personals. Pee Nut and I stayed at the motel with him until the children returned.

My daughter, who is a little Nightingale, sponged her father, gave him medicine and put him to bed.

The next morning, I took breakfast to the motel and we headed for the airport. He looked so sad and paralyzed sitting in that wheelchair. My heart went out to him. He kissed his children goodbye and kissed me also. The attendant pushed him toward the gate. We all waved goodbye.

Finally he and his wife came back from the islands. His health declined and she put him in a nursing home. To save his money she later put him in the house with one of her native friends and where his health and welfare were neglected. He didn't last long and I feel he just gave up. He passed a few days after he was placed in the hospice. To hear this condition after his passing my children can't stand to see his ex-wife when they shop at the place of her employment. He had bedsores all over his body and lost a lot of weight when he passed and was evident he suffered a great deal before passing.

Several weeks later I received a phone call from my ex-husband's wife. She knew of his employment pension and other insurance and found out that he had left everything to me. I told her I have been notified, and the checks would be sent to me. She gave me the impression that she was very letdown and disappointed about the outcome of the funds.

I suppose my ex-husband had time to put his life together. Maybe thinking of the treatment and neglect he received from his wife, my commitment in helping him go back to college, all the advantages we accomplished together, the sacrifices we made when he was near death's door and how I stuck by him when times were rough.

Being kind and helpful to a person who has been unkind to you will cause unnecessary pain and loss of goodwill.

Every day I'm confronted but many decisions where I must make that release. One must remember to first take a moment to be still and wait for the Lord's guidance for direction. When I tried to control my mind and be still, I can feel my body relaxing as tensions are eased. If you want to find peace of mind in joy in your daily activities, go to God in prayer.

I thought about attending the funeral but decided against it. He was funeralized at veteran's cemetery out of state.

My first cousin whom no one counted was one of my uncle Tom's children. Frank would always be at the house to give grandma and me a helping hand. He was very good with building and brick laying as was my Uncle Tom's trade. He looked so much like Uncle Tom, more so than his live in children. My uncle had other children scattered over town and we found out more when Frank was funeralized. Frank ended up in a nursing home and I went to see him occasionally. Just when he was heavy on my mind, I should have gone to see him but I was too late. A few days later I received the news that he had passed. He was a lonely guy but I loved him and he tried hard to please and help people. The smile on his face when I first visited him will always linger in my mind. I will never forget telling him how much he looked like his Father Tom. He only smiled and didn't say a word.

His other brothers and sisters never accepted him and although they knew all about his birth. He was never included in any will of Uncle Tom's property and I knew it was very wrong. If they didn't want me to get my mother share which was lawfully mind, you know he would be kept out if they had anything to do with it.

The funeral was very sad and the family was the majority of people attending. I told the usher to check with the pastor if I might say a few words about frank. This is what I said:

I grew up with Frank in the country. We were very close as children. I remember one summer evening I wanted a honey bun, my favorite treat. Frank said, "I'll go to the pastry store." He walked from grandma's house to the store in Nashville and walked back. He was ready to help grandma and me with anything.

When our front porch rotted away and I tried to repair it, Frank came and replaced the planks and then we painted the entire porch.

He was a faithful cousin. Grandma and I could depend upon him. I decided I didn't want a straw mattress on my bed and with my job at Marie's Grill, I got a real mattress. The mattress turned out to be too long for the bed and Frank and I cut the bed posts off. Grandma didn't like that very much.

I was closer to Frank than some of my own cousins who lived close to us.

When I went to visit Frank in the nursing home, his face lit up and I am so sorry I wasn't able to visit as much as I should have.

I love you Frank, rest in peace.

I was speaking to a friend on the phone one day and feeling so very happy and thrilled that I told her at last I had found a good man. I told her that I was in love with this man and how he makes me feel. The conversation continued about men and the bomb shell hit. She said, "You know Joseph who knows the Bible backwards and forward had women at his house. Yes, I know for a fact because I went to deliver a package to him and he always asked me in, but this morning I could hear water running and there was another car in the driveway." I almost dropped the phone but had to control myself and not let her know it was my friend she was talking about. I will never be able to express the horrible pain in my chest. If this was true, it happened long before our involvement. He told me that he hadn't been involved with anyone, so why did it affect me this way?

I find myself daydreaming of the past and I suddenly remember the experiences of despair and hurt which I experienced and can praise and rejoice in the strength I then was not aware of the inner-strength at that time—but now it is as clearly as I see the stars and the sun.

Isn't it ironic that when you are in an experience, crying your heart out, afraid to pour your heart out to a friend, only want guidance in what you should do and what you shouldn't do and you are afraid to ask? It's like being in a deep, four wall, and dark pit with no way out and then you think. God is up there! He knows how my heart aches. He wouldn't put this heavy weight on me. He has a reason for me to go through this to see if I'm strong enough to climb out. Trust I would remember my Grandma reading her Bible and quoting passages like, "Let not your heart be troubled, ye believe in me shall not perish but have everlasting life."

Trust in the Spirit within you to guide you into the most helpful ways of communicating with any given situation. We must trust the Spirit within us to unfold our life's plan and those whom we love to unfold their life plan. We will find ourselves less troubled about the future and be more peaceful about the present. If we truly have the Spirit within us, we will improve our attitudes, lighten worry, and we will be closer to the awareness of the presence of God.

My half-sister and half-brother as children were told by their mother not to associate with me and my older brother. We grew up not seeing each other after I went to visit with them as a young girl of ten. After getting married and living near them, I went to dad's house and my sister answered the door. I asked if dad was in and she said no and slammed the door in my face. Since then I only saw a glimpse of her at dad's funeral. The obituary was written by my sister and stepmother. After listing all the children, brothers, sisters, aunts, cousins, and friends, my name was at the bottom.

My brother explained to me that my sister told him she was tired of listening to her mother and since we didn't have any connection as children she would try and make up for the wrong doings we endured during childhood.

She called me and got directions to our farm house. We stayed at the farm in the summer and took care of the garden and animals. We had a very nice visit and from then on she came out of state for weekends and I would go to her home. After her third marriage she relocated in a city four hours from my home. After we caught up with our lives, I noticed that she did the things I had already accomplished. She went back to school to become a teacher, when I bought a town house; she got in debt to buy one. She saw my master's degree on the wall and she went back to school to obtain a master's degree. The last visit to my house she saw my piano and said she was taking lessons and would buy her a baby grand piano soon.

My childhood wasn't as cozy as hers. She had both a father and mother in her home and her accomplishment should have out shown mine. Deep in her mind she knew she could do everything that I did.

I remember in the late 1970's when my children were ten and twelve years old, I received a three page letter from my half-sister. I will never know to this day why she and her mother were so angry and hated me so. It was a horrible letter with words and name calling of my youngest daughter who today is a successful director. She also stated that I wouldn't get the piss from the toilet if dad died. I didn't answer the letter but took it to a lawyer and he answered it. He explained that she was breaking the law sending that type of language through the mail and if she continued, action would be taken against her. That ended that. As of this writing, I never mention her letter and I guess she thinks I have forgotten about it.

Yes, I've endured a lot of heartache and accused unjustly, but it didn't stop me from continuing to go forward and do the best that I can do and be kind and helpful to others. I was taught the Bible by my grandmother and that God knows everything and He will see us through any difficulties.

God has given me strength, courage, and determination throughout my life and with His help, I was able to instill a little motivation and desire into my students to help them to become better citizens and to go out into the world and make a difference.

Now I have met a man that has changed my life for the better. Even the world is brighter and the sun is shinier. I just love the outdoors better now than before since I'm happy. Happiness is just a word to many but not to me, because for years and years I wanted to be happy and never was. When I married, I told my husband that all I wanted from this marriage was to be happy. You never get what you wish for. After all these years it has finally happened in many ways. I just adore this man and our chemistry just goes together. We laugh, tell jokes. Being close to him I feel so alive.

He is very attentive, loving, and caring. Sometimes I ask myself is this a dream? I honestly can't believe me, Lucinda, is now happy and content. The good Lord had all of this waiting for me and I thought I didn't want anyone in my life. How wrong was I? Joseph asked me years ago to go "listen to the waves" (go to the beach). Believe me I had no idea he was serious. The gifts at Christmas came to my door from him, but yet we had no date. At church I would always get hugs. I said to Joseph later, "You must stop looking at me like that because everyone will know."

I can't wait to get up early in the morning and go outside to my patio and just look up at the beautiful sky. It is very peaceful and the little birds are chirping. I talk to God every morning outside or indoors. It's my ritual to pray every morning. I thank Him for all He has done for my family and me down the years and the blessing to have a wonderful and caring family. I pray for the community, family members, church members, and the brave people fighting to keep our country safe. Most of all I tell God how much I love Him for all the happiness He has brought into my life. For years I had the belief that love wasn't for me because I have experienced so much heartache with men.

I am learning to overlook many conditions and concentrate on the good. I try my best to let Joseph know how appreciative I am by telling him, giving him expressive cards which let him know I love him and I've tried to show it in how I treat him.

At the moment we are very much into each other. Every morning he calls when he awakes and when he returns home from his chemical plant. Usually he reads from his Bible when he's not instructing how he wants the formula developed.

I don't know what lies ahead for the two of us and maybe I don't want to know. I am living for the moment and enjoying every minute of it with him.

I'm enjoying it and will hold on as long as I have the strength.

Joseph's daughter should be proud of the care Lucinda took of her father. As soon as Joseph's daughter arrived in town and moved in, things began to change. The visits to my house became scarcer and scarcer and soon he stopped our Sunday afternoon visits. His excuse was he became sleepy. The functions we once attended now are her outings. It keeps her active since her father is her escort to these many functions.

Soon I became adjusted and got involved with other activities which kept me content. I always told him he didn't have a backbone, if so, he would stand up for himself. I guess he didn't want to hurt her jealous feelings since she is over fifty five and living with him.

We must realize that there is no fairy tale or anyone perfect but that with patience and forgiveness anyone can triumph.

Being a mother and grandmother of two beautiful daughters, seven grandchildren, and one great grandchild I am truly blessed. Not once in school or in their teens did I receive a disruptive note of bad behavior from teachers about my children. This made me very proud when they were growing up in a world of drugs, shooting, and violence.

Today my youngest daughter has traveled to twenty seven countries as an E.V.P. Director of Research and got million dollar contracts for her company. My oldest daughter, an Administrative Assistant is doing wonderful with her promotions. One grandchild has married and had a most memorable wedding—a beautiful affair.

I am bias of my older granddaughter, Lisa, who wasn't afraid to start her life's journey by working little odd jobs early in the morning before graduating from high school to enable her monetary means to attend college. She finished her college education has a good job, now working on her master's degree, first got rid of her car I gave her on her 16th birthday and doing marvelous well at this time. I'm so elated of all my grands for they have made me proud.

My journey has helped me grow as a human being and I was willing to go through more pain to get out of pain. Yes, I know I have changed because of the knowledge learned throughout the years.

Today my life is wonderful and beyond anything I could have ever imagined. Still, I ask God each and every morning to keep me in check so that I don't take any blessing in my life for granted. I will always know in the bottom of my heart that "with God all things are possible."

Some of my experiences and circumstances of my life change constantly. These changes are inevitable. I may desire them or I may wish they had never occurred.

Regardless of the changes I experience with Joseph, or anyone, I meet each one with confidence and courage. If it's overwhelming, I will rely on God's sustaining presence.

I think of II Corinthians 4:18. We look not to the things that are seen but to the things that are unseen are eternal.

Writing in my diary gave me great peace and release. I could talk freely as if to a close friend. Over the years I wrote and one day it finally came to a standstill. I am sharing some of my personal feelings with you.

January 1 Tuesday

I told my daughter if she got rid of 15 pounds by her birthday, March 17, she would get a monetary gift. I walked this morning. I feel good and spirit is high. I continue to get up between five and six am.

I asked my neighbor to come over and ring my bell. My grandma said it was good luck for a man to first come to your door on January 1. (I needed all the good luck possible). He came and we greeted each other with "Happy New Year."

January 2 Wednesday

I called to check on Olivia and went over to see her. When I got there I found out she needed things from the market. It called for snow and I felt she should get her literature "Enquirer" and essences since I don't drive in snow and ice. We went to the market and naturally I ended up with things I thought I needed.

January 3 Thursday

We awoke to our first snow. Beautiful looking at it through the window. We got between five and six inches.

Margaret, my neighbor across the street, invited me to a lovely dinner. It was a lovely affair, as I know she goes way out to have everything perfect. (We did take pictures)

My neighbor came over and cleared my driveway. He is a very thoughtful person and neighbor.

January 4 Friday

I received a lively Christmas gift from Julie, my daughter. Pleasures by Estee Lauder. I mailed a thank you and a gift. I state, "If you keep my gift, I'll keep yours". Usually when I send a check she never cashes it.

January 5 Saturday

I got up this morning praying that I make the right decision to join the Delta Sorority or not. I attended the "Rush" activity at A & T University. A time to be introduced to the procedures, pick up application and have them typed transcript from college, and recommendations from three persons other than family.

It struck me as I sat there listening and taking notes that I realized I had enough on my plate. I belong to the WIRR, WHI, sang in choir, Eti Phi Beta Sorority, Women of Universities and Colleges, Retired Teachers, Shepherds Center and others.

January 6 Sunday

I awoke up early to a cloudy morning. It called for rain and being so cold it would freeze. I wanted to attend church but decided I didn't want to take the chance of driving in ice if it did freeze.

I read my Daily Word and other readings as I do every morning and listened to the sermon by Reverend Stanly on TV. I think he is a fine minister.

Just took it easy all day.

January 7 Monday

Awoke at 5:15 put coffee on and read Daily Word and other readings. I feel good, no depression and ready to face the world.

Had an eye appointment for 9:15 which I waited over an hour because some of his staff didn't come in. My pressure was good—15 in both eyes. I pray every day I don't lose my sight. I put drops in three times a day. From the doctor's office I stopped by to see and check on Olivia and husband.

January 8 Tuesday

Up early, did my usual reading, drinking coffee, going to Margaret's house to put her newspaper at her door. Something I do daily if she doesn't beat me getting up. (I walked).

This morning I have an appointment with Dr. Cox. He is a person I can open up and talk to. I have come out of deep holes with his guidance and medication. He seemed so pleased to see me in such a happy state. I asked him how long has it been since I was last depressed? Over 1 ½ years. That's progress for me. (I hope it will continue).

January 9 Wednesday

Since I get up early morning, my doctor advised me to take a nap during the day. This I do mostly every day. Today I slept from 12 noon to 4:30 pm (I didn't know if it was morning or night when I awoke).

January 10 Thursday

Awoke early. Today is 46 days from surgery, but hate to put dye in my hair. (I wait). Walked

January 11 Friday

Awoke at 7 am (made progress sleeping a little later).

Michelle's mom Sandy made plans with me to be picked up for lunch today. Around 8am Michelle called from Cary to tell me her new infant son was not feeling well and to postpone until next Friday. Thought it was wise for it was rainy and cloudy.

I spoke with Olivia and she had to go to have blood drawn. I told her I would be there at 9:30. From the doctor's office we went by drug store to get medicine but not ready, my friend from university came over, brought beer and sandwiches.

January 12 Saturday

Awoke this Saturday morning at 5:45, did my usual reading, drinking coffee, and ran across the street to carry Margaret's newspaper. At 9:30 Jancie, my hair dresser neighbor is coming up to give me a neck trim.

I am to be at church meeting at 11 am and meet Margaret at 12:30 at Beacon Place to see our friend, Bea, who suffers with cancer. I slipped on her floor trying to get her recliner chair to lock. I sat up watching TV later in day slept approximately two hours.

January 13 Sunday

I awoke this Sunday morning around 5:15, I went to bathroom, and went back to sleep waking up around 5:45. Came in kitchen, made coffee, and read my Daily Word. I decided what meat I would have from freezer. I am still eating ham and turkey from Thanksgiving and Christmas. Went for thirty minute walk.

I am to usher in church today. Enjoyed the service and became very interested in a bus tour to New Orleans. One of the places on my list to visit. Stopped to see Olivia and she looked better than yesterday.

Closed my eyes around 4:20 pm and awoke at 6:30 pm in evening.

Printed in the United States
By Bookmasters